Nick

Thanks for keeping
the windows clean!

Hope you enjoy
reading my little cricketing
tale

Best wishes
    + Merry Christmas
Mark          2021
(the author)

# A Century, Not Out

# A Century, Not Out

## a cricketing tale

MARK RICHARDSON

*With illustrations by Jeanette Richardson and Isabella Richardson*

2021
**Charles Porter Books,**
Lincolnshire, England.

Copyright © 2021 Mark Richardson

First published by Charles Porter Books, 2021

Charles Porter Books, The Ramblers
Chapel Lane, Ashby cum Fenby
Lincolnshire, DN37 0QT

Cover design and illustrations by Jeanette Richardson and Isabella Richardson.

Should you wish to buy additional copies of this book please contact the publisher at the above address or by email to mrbooks@btinternet.com or Tel. 01472 823900.

ISBN 978-1-9196442-1-9

Printed by TJ Books Ltd.
Padstow, Cornwall.

To my father, who would have been a hundred years old on September 29<sup>th</sup>, 2021. The inspiration you gave me, the values you instilled in me, and the unconditional love with which you smothered me are treasures which I will keep for a lifetime. This book is dedicated to you.

# Preface and Acknowledgements

A CENTURY, NOT OUT, as a title, only dawned on me as I was some way through writing this short story. The working title had been, simply, The Cricket Match for the obvious reason that most of the day's events are centred round, well, a cricket match! When the title popped into my head it seemed a perfect fit as it was just the kind of upbeat cricket reference I needed, it could be blended into the story, and also the publication of the book happened to coincide with what would have been the year of my father's hundredth birthday had he lived long enough. The story, although fiction, is based on true events, a real day out and a truly glorious day's cricket. If we hadn't gone to Whiston that day, if we hadn't watched the cricket match, and spoken to some of the warm hearted folk of the village and Parish Church Cricket Club then the book would never have been written. As it was, it still took nearly three years, and the spare time given to me by a "lockdown" to protect us all from a global pandemic, for me to finally transfer the book from the images in the depths of the back of my mind onto the page. In that time the snippets of cricket knowledge I'd retained over a lifetime, merging together with the Yorkshire dialect I'd grown up with, and the influence of my wider family, were given the chance to properly form and develop into some sort of coherent whole. In the end, probably combined with a lockdown-induced lively imagination, the thoughts came flooding out in a torrent as I finally put finger tips to keyboard.

I am very grateful to the many people who have, often inadvertently, helped me in the writing of this book. Most obviously, to my wife and daughter for drawing and producing the illustrations and for putting up with me for months as I talked endlessly about the plot, imagery and dull, but necessary, production details. My dear mother, brother, sisters, teachers and friends for helping to make me the person I have become. The weird and wonderful characters who walked into my bookshop in Tonbridge over the years for providing much inspiration; obviously I can't give their names! Not to mention my other "friends" in the shop, the books! My extended Yorkshire family around the Rotherham area who, ever since I were a lad, always made me feel part-Yorkshireman even though I never lived there. They provided the inspiration for many of the characters and sayings in the book which had clearly embedded themselves into my mind. My Sister Anne should have a special mention for providing me with her thoughts on "The Bench" and for crystalizing just how much it meant for the family to maintain it. My son, Doctor Charlie, for making me such a proud dad. Most of all, thanks go to my own Dad, Charlie Richardson who, sadly, I only knew for the first half of my life but who gave me a lifetime of inspiration and treasured memories. Doesn't every son and daughter yearn to see their dads, after they've gone, for just one more day?

*The Author, June 2021*

# Contents

*"Here on our native soil we breathe once more*
*The cock that crows, the smoke that curls, the sound*
*Of bells – those boys that in yon meadow ground*
*In white-sleeve shirts are playing…"* William Wordsworth, poet.

# Prologue

FIFTY-EIGHT. That would be a half decent innings for most batsmen, but it's actually how old I'll be on Wednesday next week, and it'll be the strangest of birthdays. Due to a new virus outbreak, a pandemic, which they are saying may have been brought over by someone from China, our country has been in what is being called "lockdown" for the past six weeks. It's been like watching a dystopian movie unfold before our very eyes. The death toll has been mounting up, the hospitals are getting fuller. In this lockdown nobody is allowed out except for food shopping, essential work and exercise. Panic buying of essential supplies, even toilet paper, has become a thing. Some people do of course bend the rules, or are they guidelines? No one is quite sure when it will all end or how things will be "on the other side". Until then we must wash our hands very often; oh, and we mustn't touch our faces, especially not our mouths and eyes. It has been a weird time these past few weeks, but not all bad. My mind has had plenty of time to relax, and to drift.

On a practical note I've got loads of jobs done around our house which I'd been putting off for months, if not years; painting garage doors, staining the garden furniture, oiling the decking. The garden looks better. It's springtime but the weather has been more like mid-summer, almost in direct contrast to the news coming from our TV screens which is all very gloomy. The daffodils and tulips seem to be extra vibrant this year and we're all noticing more in our immediate surroundings.

Like some sort of a reawakening. Definitely good weather for outside jobs, and for the start of the cricket season, if only play were allowed; but the lockdown prevents it.

My dreams have certainly been more vivid and I don't think I've slept better since I was a teenager. I'm not at all sure why. Maybe it's the lack of the need to do anything, to get dressed even; paradoxically I feel freer than I can ever remember. Free to let my mind wander, as it hasn't done in years. As it needs to from time to time.

~

*"Yorker, n. Ball so bowled as to pitch immediately in front of batman's block, as introduced in Yorkshire."* The Concise Oxford Dictionary.

# The Bench

A FEW DAYS AGO, whilst proudly, but somewhat monotonously, re-painting my balcony rails at home, applying careful brushstrokes, I was daydreaming about that day last summer in Whiston, the picturesque little village on the outskirts of Rotherham, the steel town, nestling on the edge of the glorious Peak District. It was full of tough, gritty, no nonsense folk. Dad grew up there, Mum spent much time in the village, and lived there, after they'd got married in 1950. They'd take bus rides to walk in the beautiful nearby hills on summer days long ago. We'd gone, two of my sisters, my wife, brother-in-law and me to clean up and re-stain Dad's bench, there in the churchyard.

I say Dad's bench, although he never sat on it, because my Mum had had it placed in the position where it's been ever since, shortly after he'd died. It stands there, towards the back of the church yard, in clear sight of the cricket pitch. It has a brass plaque mounted on its back rest which is engraved with the words: "In loving memory of Charles Richardson 1921-1992." I like to think that Dad has been watching every match ever since from his bench. He probably has a hundred other jobs up there in Heaven but, it's a lovely thought anyway.

Afterwards we'd planned a picnic by the cricket boundary, which was lined with low fencing and various benches for the spectators who were sporadically dotted around it. As we applied teak stain to "The Bench," which is what we'd all called it ever since it had been placed there, work which was necessary as it hadn't been carried out for at least a couple of years, in the background Whiston PCCC were about to play a match on the cricket pitch just over the wall in Church Fields. The wall was somewhere between waist and chest height, so it was quite easy to keep an eye on the game from where we worked. The magnificent Norman church tower overlooked the whole scene, keeping a watchful eye on the players, as it had done for more than 200 years, ever since the club was formed. This part of Yorkshire, you might say, was cricket barmy so, even at this level, they took the match very seriously indeed. They were playing Cleethorpes, by sheer coincidence, so we had mixed loyalties since that's the town where my sisters and I grew up, but our hearts still lay in South Yorkshire as we would find out, beyond doubt, later on in the afternoon.

The account of the day's events which I'm about to tell you may sound, to some, like a fantasy but, I swear to you, this is precisely what happened, as those watching on with me will bear witness. The interpretation of just how it happened must be left for you, the reader, to decide.

~

*"Cricket has no past and no present. The seasons mingle in one another as with no other game."* Sir Neville Cardus, writer.

# The Journey

THERE WE WERE, the five of us, travelling along the motorway, the M180 just as it joins the M18. I remember the journey to Rotherham, or Rovrum, as we kids pronounced it, with a mixture of great fondness and a slight churning feeling in my stomach.

Fondness, because back in the early 1970s the journey was a very different one across countryside, through small villages, up and down dale with not a motorway in sight. I even wrote a poem as a child called "The Road to Rotherham." When Dad read it he was amazed at how much his young lad had observed about the journey. But it was the bits that I'd made up which he quoted for years to come: "…there goes a rabbit, or is it a hare?" He always said it whilst being unable to suppress his sheer delight which was, more often than not, accompanied by much rapid rubbing of his hands as only my Dad could.

The churning feeling being a mild phobia of being the passenger in a car. You see I suffered from travel sickness as a child and still do when I'm not in the driving seat. On this particular journey, in the summer of 2018, I was feeling a bit dickie as, number one, I was sitting hunched over in the back seat and, number two, I'd had more than a few glasses of a particularly agreeable rioja the night before. Now, brother-in-law Mark's Tesla back seat, however plush, and however much it felt like I was doing my bit for the environment by not travelling in my ten year old Citroen diesel, was not intended for a hung over 6'3 middle aged man that's for sure!

So there we were suddenly, or so it seemed, as I awoke from my queasy stupor, heading for Rotherham, off the M18, onto an A road; and we were soon taking the sign post for Wickersley, Brecks and, eventually, the small village of Whiston. For that was our destination.

Our mission was to repair and coat The Bench which had seen some action since it was placed there in that summer of 1992 as a sort of a shrine to my father after he'd passed away so suddenly in January, earlier that same year. It had been grafittied on, carved and written on. It had even been up-rooted and thrown through a window of the nearby church so that the thieves could gain entrance to steal some candle sticks or, more likely, just to do some mindless damage for a dare. I like to think that my Dad might have seen the funny side of this, that somehow, life was carrying on and that young tearaways would still do daft things; plus ça change and all that. I don't think my Mum saw it like that at the time though! Beside herself with fury she was.

So, anyway, there we were in Whiston village, driving past The Golden Ball, the pub where my Dad propped up the bar in his prime, telling stories about Don Bradman, Len Hutton, Brian Close and various other cricketing legends of his day. How I would've loved to have met him in his prime, in his heyday. The once spit and sawdust hostelry had long since become one of those "nice" gastro pubs where office workers and middle class families had replaced the farmers, steel workers and miners telling their tall tales and bawdy jokes. Filling the place with laughter and joy. Beyond the pub we went, and uphill to the church yard where, as a grown up, I've learnt that one half of my family history lays in the earth there. And, there it was, The Church of St Mary Magdalene with its imposing tower built of that quite depressing looking, browning Yorkshire stone which would once, presumably, have looked brilliantly white since, they say, "White Stone" is the origin of the village's name itself. There were medieval quarries in the vicinity, so we're told.

Look, I don't want you, the reader, to go thinking that this is some kind of a village history booklet, because it's not, but the information is there if you happen to be interested in that sort of thing! As far as this story is concerned, it is an impressive sight to see this large church in such a small village and to know that we'd arrived at the centre of the home village of my father and his ancestors.

We parked up by the cricket club and I stretched my back and straightened my neck after an hour and a half bent over like a rag doll in a toy chest loaded up in a removal van! We must've looked a right pair as brother-in-law, Mark, wasted no time getting his DIY clothes on; 1980s style shell suit bottoms and a very faded, paint splattered tee shirt, clearly the veteran of many previous gardening projects and paint jobs and, so I suspected, what he felt most himself wearing. I was less prepared, but had at least had the fore sight to bring my "Grumpy Old Men" apron with me, which my daughter had given to me as a joke present a few years back!  Unlike Mark though I hadn't brought any gloves with me, which I later regretted as there was sandpapering to be done. There were five of us but, since we were the only two men, both called Mark as it happened, then obviously we were about to do the bulk of the work on the bench! Along the church yard path we strolled, our minds full of thoughts about times gone by and the irreplaceable characters no longer with us. Past the dark, fading gravestones some bearing our family names.

Richardson. Porter. Abbot. Names we were all familiar with although I, being the youngest sibling, had to be reminded by my sisters of who they all were and how they were related to us. How they all fitted onto our family tree.

Down the stone path, toward the cricket boundary wall we strolled, and there it stood with its back to us. The Bench, Dad's Bench.

We'd arrived.

～

*"If it's difficult, I will do it now. If it's impossible, I will do it presently!"* Don Bradman, cricketer.

# Man's Work

YES I KNOW IT'S A BIT unchivalrous of me to say, but it did seem to me that it was taken for granted that my sisters and wife could walk off and have a chat about this, that and whatever while the two men got down to the work we'd come to do. The tin of teak stain was put to one side with the brushes and brother-in-law Mark handed me a fresh sheet of, medium coarse, glass paper which would keep me occupied for about the next hour. The mid-day sun was pretty intense on this particular afternoon in late September. No chance of bad light stopping play today, so we were going to need drinks and plenty of snacks afterwards. The ladies hadn't totally deserted us, no fear of that, they were still on hand to provide us with their expertise on how all the underside of the bench should not be overlooked and how we mustn't forget to stain the inner legs. You know, those sort of helpful tips! To be fair to her my sister, Liz, did take over brushing on some teak stain for me, oh yes, for about five minutes while I had to go off for an unavoidable natural break.

That is to say I needed to take a leak, and the only place to do it without a trek to the cricket club pavilion, was in some nearby bushes. We'd almost finished the first coat anyway and, at least, Our Liz could claim that she'd done the most important part of the job by finishing that coat! It was laborious work in the hot sun but also very satisfying knowing that we were making The Bench good for the next year or two until it'd be time to do it all over again. Mark and I ribbed each other about who was doing the most work and joked about the girls sloping off and having a lovely day while the boys did all the work. You get the idea. The truth was though that we were all enjoying ourselves in the sunshine and feeling a sense of achievement in doing this valuable work for the family. "Mum'd been reet proud!" I said to myself out loud in a corny mock-Yorkshire accent.

"Aye she would that!" echoed brother-in-law Mark in an even worse attempt at Yorkshire dialect.

~

*"Skylark: scientific name Alauda arvensis, famed for its song, the epitome of a summer's day; characteristically hovers a few feet above the ground before landing"* RSPB Pocket Guide to British Birds.

# A Serene Moment

I HARDLY EVER came to Whiston in my adult years but, you know, isn't it funny how you can feel immediately at home somewhere. And that's how it felt when I wandered off to find a secluded place to take a leak. I wandered down the path, away from the bench and looked out over the cricket pitch where lots of white figures, topped with maroon baseball caps, shimmered in the sunlight. They were bending over, running slowly back and forth and doing stretching exercises; most probably limbering up before the afternoon's knock I thought to myself. What an idyllic scene, with the sun intensifying the lush green of the outfield and the unmistakable pick, pack, puck, pock sounds of leather on willow, as the players warmed up with some practice bowls and threw the cricket ball around to each other, bringing that distinct atmosphere of an English summer's day. I've often thought that I enjoy watching sport at this grass roots level far more than the serious professionalism of the first class players. It has everything, all the passion, all the desire to win, all the banter, all the sledging and the cliff edge moments and yet you can watch it right at the boundary, for free and have a pint with the players afterwards, sometimes even during!

"Aye, champion is this!" I muttered to myself in that not very convincing Yorkshire accent again.

So there I was, trying to find a secluded spot in the bushes, still within sight of the cricket match, the first over of which had just got under way, when I realised that I was actually on a cut through from the village centre. So it wasn't that secluded after all but I just had to take a leak anyway as I was bursting by this time, but that wasn't the point. The point was that I was struck by this weird sense of being at home, belonging, of standing, pissing actually, in a spot where, quite possibly, and it feels a little indelicate to say, my father had done exactly the same thing seventy or more years previously, after a post-match session in the pavilion. It wasn't a scary moment at all, more just a little touch spiritual in a way. I'm not sure what, but I did feel something weird, nice weird, a shiver down the spine weird. But don't we often mix up that feeling of a presence when all it really might be is the wind in the trees combined with our own imaginations and emotions? What I do know though is that, as I looked across at the sun lit cricket pitch, the church and the fields beyond, I felt a serenity, a calmness I hadn't felt in many years. Along with a strong feeling, right at that moment, that I knew things would be fine, would somehow all work out. I wasn't even sure what or when, but I just knew they would. The sun shone so, so brightly that day, just looked so beautiful. A skylark hovered over nearby, singing its heart out with an unmistakable rapid tsirrup, tsiroeet call as though signalling the summer's refusal to go away, hanging on for its final flourish. If ever there was a heaven on Earth, could it be something like this?

My thoughts were broken by a loud shout from the pitch, the match which I'd not been paying that much attention to, was now in its third over:

"Howzzzzaaat?" rose out from the white figure over the boundary wall. Then a cheer. Cleethorpes had got their first wicket, the opening batsman for Whiston Parish Church Cricket Club, Wayne Crossley, had just been judged by the umpire Out LBW for three runs. It wasn't looking like a great start for the home side.

Why was I bothered though? After all, I'd only gone there to paint a bench.

~

*"In the soft grey silence, he could hear the bump of the balls.*
*And from here and from there, the sound of the cricket bats:*
*pick, pack, pock, puck. Like drops of water in a fountain,*
*falling softly in the brimming bowl."* James Joyce, writer.

# Admiring our Work

So, there it was. Looking as good as new, or very nearly. The teak stain tin empty, two coats brushed on, two men feeling a small sense of achievement. Three women feeling equally proud but also a little hot and bothered. All of us were feeling thirsty and hungry. Photos were duly taken standing alongside our work with the plaques attached to the back rest of the bench. The one for my Dad and a new one, recently added, for Mum: *"In loving memory of Barbara Richardson 1926 to 2016"* Mum had outlived Dad by more than 24 years but he'd still, kind of, always been there, at the centre of the family, and Mum had been faithful to his memory. Now they were together again, reunited or, at least, in a way us mortals could comprehend. This simple act of doing up The Bench was a symbol of the love and admiration we felt for our parents. It had done us all good to do the work. We were all proud.

A click from over the boundary wall, another mixture of shouts merging into one muddled loud one:

"Owwwisheeeee?" and Whiston's other opener, Len Braithwaite, is bowled out for 24 runs. Short lived cheering, laughing and clapping from the men in white fielding followed. It's 36 for 2, although I didn't then know the score, nor was I all that interested at this point. I was more interested in just cherishing that view over towards the cricket pitch and the fields beyond, just as my Dad told me he used to do with the Grandad I'd never known, and remembering his tales of the capers he'd got up to as a kid there.

Scrumping and pie larking about, as he would've said.

~

*"How can a ball hurt you? It's only on you for a second."*
Brian Close, England cricketer and Yorkshireman.

# That Was Close!

THE PICNIC MAT WAS LAID OUT, the sun had got its hat on and the cricketers were out to play, to paraphrase the famous song! We, on the other hand, started tucking into tuna and cucumber sarnies, and drinking our lovely sparkling chilled, very deserved, Prosecco all the way from Italy, via Lidl supermarket. The bubbles reminded me of summer afternoons in the back garden as a kid drinking our cold lemonade under the shade of the apple tree. The sun shone through the glass, emphasizing the bubbles as they floated their way up to freedom at the top.

"Do you follow cricket?" brother in law Mark asks me, while munching on a sandwich.

"Yeah, a little bit, but not really follow..." says I "...but I do like sitting and watching here when you don't have to really know what's going on. I just love the whole scene."

"But what does the 45 and the 4 mean on the scoreboard over there?" says Mark.

I think he was just feigning his total lack of knowledge of the game as I couldn't believe that an Englishman could possibly not even know the first thing about our national summer game. So I patiently began to explain that the larger number referred to the number of runs the batting team, Whiston, had scored at that precise moment and the smaller number was the cost in wickets.

"Wickets?" Mark queries.

"Come on Mark you know what wickets are! You know, the number of batsmen it's cost them to score those runs." I explain.

"So why not just call them batsmen instead of wickets. Anyway I thought the wicket was the pitch in the middle!" Mark says while grinning from ear to ear.

A realised then, of course, that he was indeed taking the micky out of me, but he did sort of have a point. Stumps, bails, wickets, pitch, bowling, googlies, Yorkers, leg spinning, silly mid-off, long leg, slips, gullies. Surely designed to confuse all but the cricket connoisseur! I hadn't thought about this for years but, it seemed, I actually knew a lot more than I'd realised I did. I had a sense of what was happening on the field of play, the players talking to one another, the captain trying to shape the field to the best advantage of that particular bowler. Or, if he knew the batsman, which was quite likely, moving his players in closer, or out longer. I'd watched enough with my mates, brother and Dad to know that much at least. It had gone in somewhere.

"Terrific sandwich. Any chance of a bit of quiche Our Anne?" says Jeanette who'd been quietly enjoying the tranquil setting, not to mention her fair share of Prosecco.

"Our Liz made it, you'd better ask her." Says Anne, not wishing to tread on any toes.

"Yes, but there is ham in it Jeanette. It's a Quiche Lorraine actually," Liz says in a mock posh voice, attempting to impersonate Hyacinth Bucket from that classic comedy series, *Keeping Up Appearances*. Yes, I think to myself, that does mean there's ham in it. Jeanette's a vegetarian you see. "Awkward!" my Mum used to say!

"I'll have another slice then Our Liz" I say, holding up my plate for her.

Ever forthright Liz says: "You are bloody greedy Mark", but I know from the grin on her face that I've paid her a big complement in obviously loving her baking so much.

"We should come here more often…" Liz says, and we all mutter our agreement between mouthfuls of sandwich, quiche, cake, biscuits, crisps and peanuts.

"…we need days like this."

"Yeah, like t' Famous Five Gooes t' Yorkshire!" Jeanette jokes with a fairly convincing accent.

"Aye and we'll need lashings of t' ginger beer next time!" adds brother-in-law Mark, followed by much laughter.

"You do make me laugh Jeanette…" says Anne, "…you are a card!"

"Blimey, that was close!" Anne gasps, and her laughter is broken, as the ball rams into the boundary fence right in front of us.

A quick glance at the scoreboard, which is being manned by a figure wearing a wide brimmed hat, umpire's-style coat and black trousers, some distance away, and who is silhouetted by the strong sun in the background, shows us that this

four by middle order batsman, Glenn Sprake, has brought Whiston's total up to
99 for 5 wickets. I watch momentarily as the home side push a loose ball for a safe
two, bringing the hundred up. There's a polite ripple of applause from the 60 or
so spectators made up mostly of players, friends and family, and club committee
members. The number on the scoreboard flips over, somewhat clumsily, to 101.
Whiston are running out of their decent batsmen but still have around half their
forty overs to build up a reasonable lead. They have to get towards 200 runs surely.

"More Prosecco Our Mark?" says Liz, tempting me with the bottle.

"Oh, go on then, being as I'm not driving!" says I. Another half glass of the still
cool bubbly drink is poured into my plastic picnic champers glass.

All very civilized, and a far cry from how things would've been in my Dad's
day I think to myself.

~

*"Cricket to us was more than play. It was a worship in the summer sun."* -Edmund Blunden, poet.

# Pavilion

THE CLUBHOUSE APPARENTLY used to be an old shed which was barely big enough to keep the equipment let alone the bar and café, changing rooms and function rooms that were there nowadays. By this time we've moved from our picnic rugs to a seating area on the terrace outside the pavilion and are told by Jane, an enthusiastic woman behind the bar, that the current clubhouse was built in the 1970s on the site of the old one but they'd been careful to make sure that part of the old "shed" remained in order to keep the character of the place. I mention that I think my Dad used to play for Whiston and she seems to immediately warm to us. She asks me when, with what can only be described as heart-warming enthusiasm, and I tell her that it was probably from the late 1930s to perhaps the late 1950s. (To be honest I wasn't that sure.) She tells me that there is an archive going back about a hundred years of players score cards and old photos and the like. At which I get very excited until I'm then told that they have been taken off to be properly catalogued and bound. I find out that I can buy a cricket cap, or these days baseball cap, from the club shop but she thinks that they've run out since it's nearly the end of the season. I make a mental note to contact the supplier which she tells me is MS Sports, Masborough Street, Rotherham.

I get the round in, mostly pints of cold IPA and refreshing lager shandy and we take up our position, sitting on the terrace outside the pavilion. I can just about make out what some of the younger players are saying.

"Tha'll never cop off wi Mel from Cow Rakes, not even 'er ugly mate wi' t' wonky nose and bad teeth!" says one guy, who's evidently one of the team's wise crackers, amid much laughter from the rest of the boys.

"What does tha know?..." says the victim of his put downs, "...anyway, I'm telling thee, I nearly pulled her in t' pub last neet..."

"Ony thing you pulled last neet was thee todger!" says one of the others, followed by much more laughter.

"I did, I were chattin her up, bought her a few drinks. She were up for it I tell thee."

"Aye, you mighta paid fo' 'er drinks all neet but tha still went 'ome wi yer sen dint yer'!" says the wise guy, and more people are in stitches.

" e'd 'ad a few pints, tha' knows but, you weren't seeing double mate...she really 'as got two 'eads!" someone else shouts out to wails of more laughter.

"Jack, come on son, wake up, get padded up, you'll be on afore long..." Bellowed Pete Maws, the Whiston coach. "Gi o'er gerrin pissed up t' neet before match and y' might 'ave yer mind on t' game!"

Jack Askew was the final batsman for Whiston and his team mate Mike Rodgers had just been bowled out for a duck. It's now 163 for 9.

"Go on Jack son... keep yer mind on t' game... forget about Mel you perv!.." come the cries of encouragement from team members, "...just whack it and clock up a few more runs... some sixes wi' any luck!"

Jack, apart from being the club's unofficial resident comedian and, therefore, fair game to be the butt end of the team's banter, was more a useful fielder and occasional bowler really, so there weren't any great expectations of his batting prowess. But he was also the sort of slogger who, on a good day, if he connected, and if he hadn't been having too much of a skin full the previous evening, could make a nice difference to the score in the last couple of overs. He'd been known to rack up a quick 30 runs and frustrate the hell out of opposition bowlers who just wanted to finish up the innings. Dwighty Evans was still at the crease as well and he was a decent middle order batsman so all was not lost though their score was somewhat low facing a good side, as we learnt Cleethorpes were.

"Gi' it some welly Jack..." more shouts to spur them on. "...come on Dwighty, a quick ton should seal it!"

Whiston are all out for 201. Dwighty and slogger Jack manage to clock up a decent extra thirty-three runs to keep the game very much alive.

~

*"Cricket and Wisden have rescued me from a lifetime of oblivion, and for that I am deeply thankful."* Aravinda de Silva, cricketer.

# Cleethorpes Innings

THE TEAMS BREAK FOR TEA in the clubhouse, a wonderful tradition for cricket clubs the world over, and they emerge a few minutes later from the pavilion. It's the visitors turn to bat.

The Whiston team take up their positions spread out over the pitch. Square leg and cover fielders move into position, and Garth Page, who is wicket keeper and also the captain, moves close in right behind the stumps after having given his directions to the team. Men spread deep at the far boundary.

"We best know what we're doin' and 'ave a plan again' this lot!" says one concerned looking Whiston spectator.

I learn that he's right, they will have to, because these openers will be tough to break.

"Right, ship 'em in then?" Says Jeanette holding up her empty glass to me. She's not paying much, if any, attention to the game but is really enjoying the day, evidently, judging by her beaming grin.

"I'll get these shall I?" says Anne. "Come with us to the bar though Our Mark." She always calls me that and it helps to distinguish between me and brother-in-law Mark of course.

So off we go inside to the relative cool of the bar area inside the pavilion. As I wait for her to order the drinks, I see photos lining the walls of teams stretching back to the 50s, and before, and some framed newspaper cuttings. But I don't suppose there are any of Dad, I murmur to myself, thinking out loud. I have a quick scan round but they're mostly too small or faded to make out faces. Even so, I'm pretty sure I'd have recognised him.

I can hear outside from the cheers of the waiting batsmen and the shouting from the middle of the pitch, that the away side are beginning to clock up some quick runs, including several fours. It's dawning on me that I'm becoming more and more interested in the outcome of the game, which is somewhat inexplicable, more so than I'd perhaps ever been bothered about any game of cricket in my whole life.

Now that's possibly not saying a great deal, as I've already explained I'm not exactly a cricket connoisseur, but I was beginning to feel a real sense of belonging and desire for the home side, my home side, to get a win. It could've been just as simple as that. I like sport, on the TV or live and I could probably get into crown green bowling if I watched it long enough, but this was somehow different. I just sensed that it was.

Back out on the terrace I could see how busy the score keeper was, that shadowy figure some distance away, as he hastily flicked over the old metal number plates which now showed that Cleethorpes were already 44 for no wickets with only three overs played. That 201 of Whiston's was starting to look like it might be a breeze. But, anything can happen in sport as we all know. A match could swing on one really good over from a team's pace bowler or spinner. And in Peaty Nicholson and Pal Panesar Whiston had a couple of bowlers who, on a good day, could make a difference. The youngster, Nick Forth, could also swing the ball really finely, on a good day but, like all players still learning their craft, he was inconsistent and probably too risky to try out in this game. We learnt all of this from the groundsman, come club manager, come unofficial Second Eleven coach, Carl Davidson who, having been told by the bar staff that we were returning Whiston folk, warmed to us and filled us in, whether we wanted it or not, on some of the finer points and team tactics. Peaty for example liked to put a fielder at deep fine leg so that he could tempt the batsman into a wild swing at an apparent short ball. It had caught many a tail-ender out by all accounts.

Trouble was these were not tail-enders and the Cleethorpes openers were two of the most experienced hitters in the region. One of them had had a brief spell for Nottingham some years back.

"Bloody 'ell lads get in tighter and concentrate or we've 'ad it." Came one cry from an increasingly frustrated local fan sitting on a bench on the nearby boundary.

"Come on then Beefy, sup up," says Jeanette, mockingly to me, I think she was referring to Ian Botham, or it could have been the amount of food I'd eaten at our picnic! "…we've still got to get back you know."

"Yes, but we can stay to watch at least till we know it's out of reach, can't we?" I plead. Cleethorpes were now 89 for none.

"I reckon another 50 runs at this rate and we can call it done and dusted." I explain. But really I knew deep down, by this time, that I had to stay to see the game out whatever the result.

"Yeeeees!..." a cry from groundsman Carl goes up, "...he's gone and bowled 'im!"

I look up and sure enough, the stumps are flying like skittles and the bails are spinning in the air, glinting in the sun light as they do. I see all this, almost in slow motion, as though watching the TV replay, which seems odd looking back on it, but that's how it was to me at the time. The Whiston players on the pitch and Carl, standing alongside us, are punching the air and the players congregate in the centre of the pitch for several seconds whilst the new batsman walks on.

It's 94 for 1 and there is now at least a glimmer of hope.

Our Anne, Liz and Jeanette have given up on the idea of going back home any time soon and have retaken their position back on the picnic rug at this point, a little back from the field of play. I can make out Anne laying back and, as she often does, helped by the Italian fizzy wine no doubt, falling into a late afternoon snooze. Her father's daughter alright!

∼

*"And o'er the grassy surface sweeps; with bended knee the batsman keeps a forward stance, to watch its way and mark it rise then sans delay his arms descend with lightning fall to smite again the ringing ball."* William Goldwyn, schoolmaster.

# Peaty Goes Down

"Not looking great is it!" says our enthusiastic bar woman, Jane, as she wanders round collecting the dead glasses from the tables on the terrace. It turns out that Jane is Peaty the bowler's wife. Peaty is so called, not only because his name is Pete, which it happens to be, but also because he is manager at the Rotherham branch of B&Q in charge gardening products, including peat I guess! Come on, you didn't expect him to be a steel worker did you? No one does that anymore!

"I'd have put money on us giving 'em a good showing today…" she says while shrugging her shoulders, "…but I'm playing a much more important game tomorrow any road…" She says unconvincingly. It's the ladies match against Kilnhurst on Sunday she tells us, and Jane Nicholson happens to be Whiston's captain and top batter.

"Come on Peaty!" She yells some much needed encouragement at her husband who looks over from the field with a frustrated grimace.

The game moves along.

Good knock. Two runs.

The umpire's arms are in the air. A brilliant six goes sky high, over the spectators and almost into the cow field some twenty yards beyond the boundary on the off side.

There's more cheering from the away batters as their opener and batsman number three clock up an impressive score between them.

Another quick one and the Cleethorpes main batsman, still stubbornly at the crease, clocks up his hundred. No mean feat at this level. Applause ripples all round.

It's 127 for 1 and it's starting to look inevitable for the home side. There's a feeling, which you can almost touch, of the coming gloom. The momentum is most definitely with the away team.

Another three runs, as they hit the ball deep, and it lingers inside the boundary rope as the fielder gives chase and throws back short.

"Come on boys, don't just gi' up. Pride in the team lads. Go to t' last over!" shouts Jane from near us.

"Yeah, and it soon will be over!" one Cleethorpes player crows, very un-cricket like, followed by slightly embarrassed, stifled sniggering from the others on the bench.

Then there's a click, more of a crack actually, from the centre of the pitch, which you can even hear from the pavilion. Like the snapping of a twig. And Peaty goes down holding his leg.

"Fucks sake, shit, shit…" he's squealing in agony.

As it transpires, Peaty Nicholson has stepped into a dip in the ground on the outfield during his run up, twisted his ankle and fractured the fourth metatarsal bone in his left foot. There's no getting round it, he's got to go off. His wife Jane comes on to help and they all wait for the ambulance to arrive and tell him to stop being a girl, amid his moaning noises.

"Hey, less o' that!" Jane shouts at them, "You can see he's 'urt, stop it all on yer!"

They all know really that it's fairly serious and that it's quite a good job the season is nearly done, as Peaty is probably the most impressive bowler Whiston have had in years.

Umpire Nick Jennings steps forward and, twiddling with the end of his handle bar moustache, waits until the fuss has died down a bit. He's old-school, takes no nonsense; but is also a fair man who's played lots of cricket in his day and, since retiring from playing at the tender age of 62, has seen all the tricks. So he doesn't miss a lot.

"Now gentlemen…." he bellows in his near baritone voice, turning to the Whiston players, "…do you 'ave a replacement?" They all look to the clubhouse but twelfth man Gordon Pattison is nowhere to be seen.

"Bollocks! where's Gord?" someone pipes up.

Gordon's not a bad bowler, useless batsman but, on a good day, can really make that ball move, especially late in the day. The team could do with him right now. The message comes out that he had to go home as one of his kids had been in a fight and was in a bit of a state. He'd presumed that he wouldn't be needed at this late stage in the match.

"Fabulous, that's us stuffed then!" says one helpful player.

"Just stay calm everyone," says captain Garth, "…we'll sort summat out." But his face is telling a different story.

"Any volunteers? Come on we'll tek' anyone" Jack Askew says in a mockingly pleading tone, as though performing theatrically to the crowd, and to much amusement but, perhaps, this time he's not joking.

And that's when something quite strange and remarkable happened.

~

*"Don't stop chasing your dreams, as dreams do come true."* Sachin Tendulkar, cricketer.

# Call Me Chaz

"FLIPPIN' 'ECK, IS IT BOBBY CHARLTON?" quips some wise guy on the Cleethorpes bench when they see the man jogging with purpose down the steps from the pavilion. He cuts an unlikely saviour figure on first glance. With his old cricket attire, which looks as though it might have been rediscovered in the lost property box. But, on closer inspection, he's actually very smartly turned out. He's about 5 foot 11 inches tall and pretty lean looking. The sleeves of his white shirt are rolled up neatly like he means business and they reveal his strong looking, sinewy forearms which are tanned like his face. He's ruggedly handsome in a traditional sort of way, his teeth are gleaming white and there's just a flash of an old Hollywood movie star look about him. His immaculately white Oxford bags-style trousers have perfectly pressed turn ups and pleats. His old fashioned looking, spotlessly white cricket boots clack as they hit the wooden steps on his way down from the pavilion. The thin strands of hair on the top of his head fly in the breeze as he jogs towards the crease. He pauses and looks up to the sky, sun on his face as if taking it all in and maybe psyching himself up, before pulling on his maroon Whiston PCCC cap. I don't see his face at this point but catch a glimpse of him as he almost brushes past me running away toward the pitch, close enough for me to feel a waft of the air he's displaced and to smell his Old Spice aftershave. I suppose that any man of a certain age would know that aroma anywhere, wouldn't they! That same weird tingle goes down my spine just like it did earlier in the day in the bushes. Somehow, I just sensed that this could be the pivotal moment in the game, that everything would be okay. But, maybe, that was just simply my heart ruling my head though. He waits patiently at the boundary with his back towards me, briefly glancing back to where we're sitting.

The sun is glinting through the trees bordering the fields, casting beams of light and long shadows.

Getting towards the close of play.

Whiston just wanted to see the game out and, to have a fair crack, they needed a full team. Both umpires and both captains had to agree to this player being allowed to take part. He had, after all, come out of the pavilion, and was wearing his Whiston cricket club cap and so, after much discussion, they did agree on the grounds that he was obviously a local and, anyway, the game was all but lost so what harm could it do? Captain Garth Page's combination of persuasion and begging with them, and promising to buy them a couple of pints after the game, may also have helped!

So, after a brief word with the score keeper, and the Cleethorpes captain, on he came. He certainly had the appearance of a cricketer about him but there was also something quite different about the way he carried himself, that's for sure. He looked like the product of a different cricketing age in his baggy legged white trousers, dress shirt with rolled up sleeves, big round white shoes and flat cricket cap which was like one of those I remembered when watching the older players in test matches on the telly in the 1970s. These, I'm told, have made a bit of a comeback among some players who like the retro look. On him though it was just the perfect way to finish off his look. He'd remove it every so often to straighten his hair and mop his brow. You could see, even from where I was standing at the far side of the pitch, why some of the Cleethorpes team's wise crackers had been ribbing him with the Bobby Charlton jibes. His side parting had crept down so that his hair on top could be swept over to cover his baldness and, even from a distance away, you could tell by the way he kept brushing it aside with his hand, that he was slightly self-conscious about this. He ran over to captain Page, who was wicket keeper as well, to get his instructions.

"Can tha' bowl?" Garth asks him, almost pleading. "We're a bit short on 'em today as you might 'ave guessed!"

"It's been a while but I used to be quite handy!" He winked and smirked with a cheeky, friendly but almost arrogant grin which might just have suggested "just watch and learn son." You couldn't put your finger on it but that little smirk of his just oozed confidence, but wasn't at all threatening, in fact quite the opposite.

"Can we please resume play gentlemen…" bellows Umpire Jennings whilst looking at his watch, "…some of us, me included, want to get 'ome afore midneet!"

And play resumes with spinner Panesar, tossing the ball from the back of his palm and catching it again, in preparation, sort of practicing his technique at close range, as only spin bowlers can.

Cleethorpes clock up another boundary, then another two, and then a quick single. Then there's a shout, an appeal, almost a desperate plea, from Panesar and the close fielders as their number three batsman slightly edges it to the keeper.

A gasp from the now growing number of spectators, who are paying far more interest than they were twenty minutes before. A pause, which seems like an hour long, then the umpire's finger goes up.

"Come on boys, we can do this…" says an old fella at the boundary, getting a bit over excited. Some of the rest of the crowd nearby him laugh at this but this old fella is, perhaps, the one sensing a slight shift in the momentum of the game.

It's 143 for 2. But surely now it's not going to happen for the home side. Is it?

"Right then Bobby Charlton…" says Captain Garth, tossing the mystery new player the now somewhat worn and scratched ball as the players change ends for the next over, "…show us yer worst!"

The Cleethorpes batsman lines up with the umpire.

"Two please sir" he shouts down the wicket; and the umpire indicates when he's lined up his bat.

Our new mysterious bowler, eagerly watched by the home crowd, takes a long run-up down the leg side that even Bob Willis might have been proud of; and there's a thud as the ball whacks into the Cleethorpes opener's pad. There's no shout for lbw though, as it's fairly plain that the ball wouldn't have hit the stumps, but the delivery shows definite promise.

"Nice try old fella…" says the batter, "…not close though, maybe you're past it mate"

There's that smirk again from our mystery new bowler. This time it sort of says "Okay, you got me there but that was me being a bit rusty and sizing you up."

Next ball comes down. But it's wide. A sigh comes from the crowd, with growing frustration.

"That's it…" calls one "…we're reet buggered now!"

Everyone around him either laughs or says in unison, "Shut thee gob. Gi' 'im a chance."

"No ball, cries the umpire" and Cleethorpes rack up another run getting ever closer to that 201 they need with plenty of balls remaining.

In the distance from where me and brother-in-law Mark are still sitting, still supping cold lagers on the terrace, I can make out that our mysterious new player is rubbing the smooth side of the ball very briskly on the inside of his trousers' thigh, in the hope that this old trick will shine the ball enough to create some movement. There's a little cloud cover developing which may help, who knows. At least it gave us some more hope.

He runs up and, as he's level with the crease on the leg side, his arm whirls over and there's a tiny flick of his wrist as he releases the ball.

The next thing the Cleethorpes opener sees is his off stump uprooted, clean out, and the bail on that side spins delightfully in the air as if it's being held there for the cameras to get a good shot. The other bail just stays put as the umpire shows no hesitation in raising his finger to signal that he's out.

145 for 3 and things are getting just a little interesting.

Sleepy eyed spectators have started sitting a bit closer to the front of their seats but daren't allow themselves to get too hopeful. Some of them though, can feel it in their guts. The momentum had begun to swing in our favour. Just a touch, but it was there and sometimes that's all you need, isn't it? But was there still time? A quick look at the scoreboard again which shows that there are still 9 overs remaining and they need to get 57 runs from them. With the quality batsmen of this Cleethorpes side it should be just a matter of time.

"You 'ave done a bit of bowling before 'aven't you! Good over old fella. Just the lift we need…." says the Captain Page. Then, turning to Panesar quietly says, "… now Pal mate just slow it down, contain 'em, stop 'em getting big 'its as much as yer can…." He then swings round to the rest of the team to give instructions, "Right lads you come in and Regsy, out much further nice and deep"

New life had been breathed into the Whiston team.

"What's yer name again old fella?…" says the captain to our mystery player.

"Call me Chaz…" He says "…and, less o' t' OLD!" And there's that little friendly smirk again. When Garth Page looks at Chaz more closely he sees that he isn't actually that old as it happens, perhaps late 30s, maybe early 40s, which I suppose is old compared to some of the younger lads in the Whiston side but Garth is 36 himself. It's just that there was something old, or more accurately, olden about him. Was it the baggy whites, the hair swept over, the immaculately clean cricket boots? Or maybe just his overall gait and the way he held the ball, held himself. He had a presence, a calming influence that silently said: "We can do this boys if we just dig deep and grasp this moment, believe in yourselves."

Garth, whose father and grandfather had also been called this unusual first name, had developed an instant liking for Chaz, almost as though they'd been friends all their lives. He watches, still a little mystified, as Chaz jogs over to the deep covers, the opposite side of the field from where we're sitting. Panesar lines up for his short deceptive run up.

~

*"Sledging: Verbally intimidating the opposing player to gain an advantage/A humorous attempt at distraction. Esp. in cricket."*

# The Spinner's Over

PALVINDER PANESAR is perhaps 24 years old, he's wearing a sporty black patka with his hair all bunched inside it, up towards the back of his head. He looks every inch the spin bowler as he tosses the ball, nonchalantly, out of the back of his hand. He's eyeing up the Cleethorpes batsman as he comes in for the first ball of his over. Ooh!...and it's a close thing as the batsman raises his bat, slightly misjudging the spin as it comes in towards his off stump, missing it by a whisker.

"Don't take any chances Rob…" comes the shout from the Cleethorpes bench, "…keep it tight and we've got this in the bag."

Next ball comes in from Panesar and Rob pushes it for a quick single. Then a two and another single from the next two balls. Then a no ball, which goes off the batsmen's pad, all the way to the boundary for 4 more. Cleethorpes are riding their luck a little but they have the advantage. A costly three to the outfield and then a tight ball is defended. Not the worst over but the opposition team have pushed the score on. A little ripple of applause goes round as they change ends for a new over.

"Nice one Pally," shouts the Captain in encouragement. "We can still do this, let's go till t' last ball…bit of pride now." His voice sounds that little bit less convincing though as time, the runs and the overs tick by. It's 154 for 3 with 7 overs remaining. Cleethorpes need 47 runs for the win, as they have wickets in hand.

"Come on…" I say, leaving my seat "…let's get down to the boundary." I almost jog down there, not really noticing Mark following me because now I'm so deeply into the game and fully focussed on Whiston achieving something special, I'm sort of entranced by it all and I can't really explain this extraordinary feeling. My love of sport? Sense of belonging, or something else? It's going to be a close game and you can feel the excitement rippling around the ground. Some kids from the surrounding streets have heard what's going on and have streamed onto the fields beyond the far boundary. Half of Cow Rakes Lane and folk from Moorhouse, Hungerhills and all over the place, it seems, have come along to see the closing of this game. There must be hundreds of them.

~

*"Batsmen can spend a whole lifetime finding the one- that bat which suits their style to perfection."* Anon, journalist.

# Chaz's Second Over

CHAZ IS TOSSED THE BALL by the wicket keeper and captain. "Come on Chaz mate this one's gunna be crucial. No pressure, just gi' it yer best mate..." says Garth Page, while clapping his hands together vigorously for encouragement, "...do it fo' Whiston!"

An older fellow in the crowd, yes it has definitely become a crowd now, peers over at Chaz and tries to get a good look at his face, but he's a bit too far away to properly make him out.

"Reminds me of someone who played here when I were a lad..." he's momentarily confused, "Naa, it couldn't be him though, maybe one of his nephews or grand kids or summat, but, naa, that were 60 year ago, must be at least." He ponders on this for a few seconds, and then his mind refocuses on the match.

I'm just leaning on the fence totally enraptured, but I do notice that Chaz, bowling from the bottom end, does cut an unusual figure and there's something friendly, perhaps even familiar about him. This look of familiarity I notice but I'm too into the game to really clock it. That comes later when I'm thinking about things after the end of the match. But here we go, on with the game.

Chaz is coming in for his next ball, cap off now, sleeves rolled up. The hair on the top of his head drops from the side parting Bobby Charlton style, and flies around as he runs in. He's distracted by someone in the crowd in the corner of his eye, a smart young lady people recalled later, as his arm whips over.

"No ball" Cries the umpire, standing behind the stumps. Chaz has overrun and it's given Cleethorpes a precious run. He marks the line of the crease, in frustration, by scratching it with the spikes of his right boot, making sure the same doesn't happen on the next ball.

Then he puts in a faster bowl, my gosh it's fast, but it's short and the experienced Cleethorpes batsman knows how to deal with this one and catches it perfectly on the sweet spot of his bat, knocking it almost out of the ground for six. The umpire's arms go up and there's a sigh of disappointment around the pitch from the Whiston fans. Meanwhile a massive cheer goes up from the Cleethorpes bench as they all jump up in unison

"Come on lads' let's 'ave 'em!" They cry, whilst spontaneously raising their arms and pumping their fists.

Chaz looks sideways at Garth, the captain, and winks at him. A couple of the other players close in notice this and are not quite sure what to make of it. Surely he's not so self-confident, so swaggering, as to deliberately lead them into thinking they can hit him out of the ground, is he?

At any rate the next ball comes in and they push it for a two. Then they hit a single off the next ball. A full toss off the next is hit for another two. Then Chaz lines up for the last ball of the over, which has shown promise but has also been a little sloppy in places.

"I said it's been a while," says Chaz, almost like he's speaking aside to the audience. His run in for this last ball is a little longer than for the other five.

The batsman, Pettigrew, watches the bowler's every move like a hawk as he pats his bat against the crease in readiness. He feels his fingers lightly gripping around the familiar handle. He can feel the perfect balance of his trusty bat. But he was no match for this delivery.

"Yeeees!.. " goes the cry all around the boundary and Chaz has clean bowled their best batsman, Robert Pettigrew.

"He used to play fo' Notts y' know." Cries one excited old fella in the crowd.

And he had, about ten years ago, he was very promising but a dodgy knee had cut his career in the big time short. At this level though he was almost invincible. Or so it seemed to many a minor leagues bowler!

But not this time.

～

*"I don't like cricket, (Oh, no) I love it..."* Graham Gouldman and
Eric Stewart, singer/songwriters.

# Old Head on Young Shoulders

"Bloody fantastic!" says captain Page as Chaz slowly jogs backwards, modestly, towards the far boundary again. He shouts encouragement to some of the other players and smirks again with even more confidence.

But surely this confidence is still a little premature? Granted, he got their best batsman out in fine style but the score is still in Cleethorpes favour. It's 166 for 4 and Cleethorpes are getting close to their target of 201. They need 35 runs to win and could even do it on the next over; and Whiston are going to have to go for the win with a different bowler as the rules say that each bowler can have a maximum of eight overs and Pal Panesar has had all of his eight. So captain Page mulls over whether to call on some young talent, which is always a bit risky at any stage in the game, but at this stage? As it becomes clear that he is giving young Nick Forth the nod for the next over a ripple of discussion and shaking of heads goes around the ground, like a Mexican wave, but he has little choice, what with injuries and the more experienced bowlers already having had their overs. And he has a feeling, and it is only a feeling, that young Nick Forth, who has an old head on young shoulders, can put together a decent over if only he can hold his nerve.

"Go on lad..." Keep it tight." Garth says while holding Nick's head in his hands on either side, as though to emphasize the need to stay focussed.

"Look at me..." says Page, "just concentrate, lose the nerves, you can do this," he says, using words of encouragement which do help, but also serve to pile on a bit of extra pressure on young Forth.

If only Nick hadn't been up till 3 o'clock in the morning partying with his mates, and wasn't feeling quite so groggy, then he might have had his eye in a bit more.

He needed to wake up, and quick, if he wasn't going to let his team down. Perhaps though, if he hadn't felt so rough, he'd have been more nervous than he was and the pressure might have been too much for him.

"You look knackered mate!" says the Cleethorpes batsman at the bowler's end, seeing his hung over pale face close up, ribbing him, he knows it might help put him off just enough. It's all part of the game!

"That's enough of that," says Umpire Jennings to nip the sledging in the bud; he's starting to dream of his cool after-game pint and can't wait to unload the five or six player's jumpers he's wearing around his waist and over his shoulders. It's been a hot day, but it's starting to cloud over a bit, as the shadow of the church tower is cast over the pitch, as if reminding them of how late in the day it was and maybe serving to provide some kind of divine inspiration at the same time.

Forth comes in from the top end, but it's well short and hammered for four runs to the leg boundary. Umpire Jennings waves his arm, to indicate a four to the score keeper at the board. Cleethorpes move closer with only 31 to hit. They start to feel the win in their veins. Then they hit a quick single, then a two. There's an edge off the next ball, which the captain dives for, and it tantalisingly shaves off his outstretched glove, but goes deep to the boundary. Chaz, picks up and returns the ball at pace to the wicket keeper as they try for the third run. But they're not quick enough and Edgerton, Cleethorpes number 5 batsman is run out for 54, stumped by Page.

A roar of delight, mixed with testosterone-fuelled thumping of the air and grunts of encouragement comes from the crowd, which must have grown to a few hundred, possibly even a thousand strong. Where they'd all come from was anyone's guess.

"Good innings Matty…" the cry goes up from the Cleethorpes bench. "…come on guys keep calm, plenty of balls left to knock a few more for the win…" those sort of noises. But the crowd, who are right behind Whiston, willing them along, can sense that the visitors are rattled. It's 183 for 5 and Whiston are going to have to bowl them out really to stand any chance of winning. But, come on, 5 wickets in two overs, is that really possible?

In the crowd some of the kids are messing about, but most are watching through their fingers, with their hands covering their faces, such is the tension.

"We're gunna lose again….they're too experienced to chuck this 'un away…this old fella …he'll be knocked art t' park, Course 'e will… come on Whiston g' f'it!" Come the cries from all around the field as the clouds come over again.

"Great conditions for swing bowlers?" a few onlookers think to themselves.

~

*"When summer's done, the game's not gone- There's Cricket on the Hearth!"* Norman Rowland Gale, poet.

# Chaz's Final Over

CHAZ IS STANDING IN THE FAR DISTANCE, bowling from the bottom end, with his longest run up yet, reminiscent of Michael Holding in his prime! He's looking up at the sky and up to the top of the church tower. Is it for some divine help? Or maybe to assess the conditions, who knows, but it added to the tension. He smiles to himself, enjoying the moment, calls something to the captain and the field is moved around, tweaked really. A slip fielder takes up his position alongside the keeper. And Chaz starts his run. He comes level with the stumps and his arm whips over, the strands of hair on the top of his head flying to the side, revealing his baldness and adding to that dashing look of Bobby Charlton in full athletic flight. If Sir Bobby had played cricket, surely this is what he'd have looked like! It's a quite stunning delivery, an out-swinger which catches his man unawares and he nicks it, but it's wide of the slip fielder and goes deep to the boundary. The deep square leg fielder gathers the ball and fields it well. Keeping it tight for two runs. Cleethorpes need 16 more runs to win the match. The tension is almost tangible.

The next ball comes in and, this time, it's an in-swinger which catches the batsman off guard. He can only push it but it spins into the air. Chaz runs in and gathers the ball with a safe pair of hands.

"Yeeeees! He's caught and bowled 'im...Fantastic!...If only we had this sort of excitement every Saturday ...I'd come daan 'ere all' t' time!" come the comments in the crowd. Even more people crowd into the ground as word had clearly got out, round the village. There are people streaming into the grounds from the gaps in the hedges and the fence, and from the church yard.

The spectators must now be five or six deep all around the boundary fence. Some are chanting his name:

"Come on Chaz, do it fo' team, fo' Whiston…" shouts one
"Chazz-er, Chazz-er, come on Chaz…" chant some others.
"Come on lad, you can do it…" screams another.

They seem to know him or, perhaps, maybe they're just getting carried away in the moment. It had become a very exciting finale after all.

Mark and I look at each other in amazement momentarily, in joint recognition of witnessing something really quite special as we watch, enraptured, from our ring-side position on the boundary fence.

Chaz is running in for his third bowl of his final over. He knows that, if the game goes to another over Cleethorpes could whack the ball for six off any loose ball from young Forth, so this is it, it has to be now. The cloud cover is just right. He runs in and delivers another beauty, another in-swinging ball which whacks against the batsman's pads, the whole team and half the crowd scream at the umpire, appealing for lbw. There's a brief pause before his finger goes straight up to indicate his decision. Chaz puts one arm in the air in triumph and smiles with a huge grin, while rubbing his hands together. But he quickly settles again to concentrate on the next batsman who he briefly sizes up as the tailender walks out, slightly hurriedly, still doing up his pads. The people in the crowd are stunned by the sheer perfection of that deliver and, more importantly, so are Cleethorpes who are now down to their last really decent middle order batter, who's looking rather worried as he does not yet have strike. It's 185 for 7 now. Cleethorpes are still favourites if they hold their nerve.

Chaz goes over to the captain Garth Page and indicates his thoughts about fielding position changes and the captain moves some of the outfielders around, with the slip moving out a little wider. Chaz looks up at the clouds again, at the church tower, at the crowds around Church Fields; a bigger smirk shows on his face, as he brushes his hair to the side with his hand, rubs a little grease into the ball and gives it a right good shine, (all within the rules surely!) Then he starts his long run in, with almost a little shimmy this time, as he comes into the crease, a subtle change of footwork and a twist of his wrist, the arm whips round again. The ball seems to move in the air first in, then out, it catches the bat, as the batsman tries to pull his shot. Off it goes hurtling towards the slip fielder, who catches the ball with both hands as he dives to his right, as though The Ashes themselves depends upon it! Everyone cheers and is slightly awestruck, patting Chaz on the back. High fives all around. All very modern!

"Come on Whiston, I knew you 'ad it in you…" cries the spectator, who had been writing them off only twenty minutes previously!

Chaz has two balls of his last over remaining. It's 185 for 7. But Cleethorpes know that they can win it on the next over if they can just get a couple of runs from this one. There's much anticipation for the next ball as Chaz runs in.

Some in the crowd hear a young woman's excited voice shouting to him; words of encouragement, perhaps? No one can quite hear above the general noise of an excited crowd. Does she distract him? A slight lapse of concentration perhaps. The next ball goes wide and off to the deep boundary on the off side. To make matters worse, it's over fielded and the away side grab another two sneaky runs to make the score 189 for 7. They only require 12 runs for the win, a win which is expected of them. Chaz still has two balls but won't have enough to bowl them all out, and the Cleethorpes batsman know this. Robinson, the best remaining batsman, has a quick word in the middle with his fellow batsman and it's clear that he wants to regain strike on the next ball so that he has it at the start of the new over. Chaz indicates, from afar, that he wants a fielder close in at square and they move about like a team with knew confidence, like birds of prey ready for their meal.

The crowd are almost silent now as Chaz runs in, it swings again viciously and is long, coming in to the middle stump, taking it out cleanly. Lots of arms go up in the air again all over the pitch. A roar goes up from the, by now, twelve hundred fans around the boundary fence and I can feel my heart racing. I've not felt this elated, this alive, this excited, since I stumped the best batsman as a nine year old kid playing on the school fields at the back of my house with my big brother and the boys from the neighbourhood.

189 for 8, with 1.1 overs remaining, it tells us up on the score board. Even the score keeper, that shadowy figure, just visible, now sitting in his little hutch beyond the far boundary, can be seen leaping up in excitement.

Chaz has one ball left of his over and then it's down to the youngster, Forth, to pick up the last two wickets. He's facing Cleethorpes tail ender Rob Jones, who had been known to whack a few in his time. But he is no match for what comes next from Our Chaz. He comes around the wicket and, this time, his run up is shorter and slower and the ball less shined. The clouds had parted slightly to allow a glint of sunshine to come through the middle giving the whole scene a kind of Heavenly appearance. The swing on the ball of this fine delivery is almost unbelievable, seeming to defy the laws of physics. It swings, first, from left to right, and then it swings back again. A proper googly you might say, if that were possible for a pace bowler. The crowd, and me included, watch it swing from one side to the other, and this time we all see it as if in slow motion. We will it to hit the target. The batsman tries to follow the ball in the air but can only push his bat down to prevent the ball getting underneath him, but the ball thuds instead onto his glove and goes off sideways. The fielder, who had been deep on the off side is quick to notice what's happening and comes running in at full pelt. Diving out in front of him, and catching the ball low, almost on the ground with both hands. The whole team are now playing out of their skins.

"Owwwwzat??!!" A massive shout goes up from the Whiston players, all except Chaz who just looks knowingly, with that confident smile of his and the umpire gives it. Chaz's arm goes up again, with that grinning face showing his brilliant white teeth. He rubs his hands together in utter delight. The home players all come into a huddle briefly to savour the moment.

"Out!" says the umpire, with his finger outstretched, and the game is poised for the final over at 189 for 9. Whiston need 1 more wicket, Cleethorpes need 12 more runs. They hoped to be in a better position going into this over but Robinson has strike and Young Forth is inexperienced and hung over.

*"The true test of any cricketer's character is how he reacts when the going gets tough, when it's time to dig in."* Michael Holding, cricketer.

# Go Forth

GARTH, THE CAPTAIN, has a word with young Nick as they change ends. "Down to you lad, just do your best, try not to feel the pressure, do it for the crowd, seeya, look at 'em all o'er there, there's thousands on 'em counting on ya." He's trying to ease the pressure that's been placed on these young shoulders of Nick's but only makes it worst for him. And it really does seem to Nick like there are thousands of fans looking on as well. The Cleethorpes batsman, Robinson, who'd overheard what Garth Page was saying, joins in ribbing young Forth,

"Yeah, come on Nicky lad, do it for your home crowd, you'll never get this many people watching you again probably ever. No pressure mate, ha, ha!" As I say this kind of talk, sledging as it's known, was part of the game and should surely be allowed in the rule book!

"Fuck off Robbo…" says captain Garth "…gi' young lad a chance!"

"Now come on lads…" says umpire Jennings "..it's been a clean game up to now, let's not ruin it at the last…keep your 'eads… Play"

Forth walks away from the stumps at the pavilion end, Chaz is standing deeper, behind young Nick, almost on the boundary. There's a little encouraging wink from Chaz to Nick as he turns to line up for his run up. He smiles, a little nervously, holding the ball on the seam. In he comes and there's a little movement in the air still. But the ball is a bit loose and is declared a wide by the Umpire. 11 runs needed for the win.

"Come on Nicky lad," comes a shout from the edge of the pitch from an old fella sitting on a pitch side bench. "Do it fo' Whiston…"

He walks away, shining the ball as he does, and turns again to run up. His next ball comes down to Robinson who hits it clean, pushing it to the off side for two and, crucially, keeping strike. 9 runs required.

Nick Forth shakes his head, slaps both his cheeks frantically, as if to wake himself up and find the energy, the courage. Chaz nods to him with a signal to send it to the batsman's right. Forth comes in with added gusto, delivering an outswinging ball, wonderfully tantalising, to the batsman's right but it's not enough to fool this wily batter, with his trusty bat which he'd, no doubt, chosen as carefully as Harry Potter chose his elder wand! Robinson hits a majestic cover drive for another two runs and the deep cover fielder gathers and returns the ball safely to the keeper. Cleethorpes need seven, they're going to have to go for it now with only four balls remaining of their forty overs.

With the next ball, Forth tries the same thing, but Robinson is on to him and contacts with the bat, good and hard, with a beautiful "pock" sound which echoes around the place as the fans hold their heads in their hands. Four runs are added to their score. The Whiston fans can hardly watch. Now their opponents need just three runs from three balls. It could hardly be a more exciting finish. It's been pulled from nothing, with this new star player Chaz's help, who came from the pavilion as a replacement for Peaty, the injured bowler, but it still looks like it may have been for nothing. Will Forth be able to stay calm and finish the job? At the far end some in the crowd notice that Chaz has come in to speak to young Nick Forth. Probably words of encouragement from an older player. Maybe some tactics. Mark and I, together with the thousands of fans around the ground, watch on for the thrilling finale, hardly daring to breath. Chaz pats young Nick on the back and rubs his hair almost like he would a young child he's proud of. "Go on son, you've nothing to lose if you do what I've said." He seems to be saying. He winks once more, smiles and shakes his fist in encouragement.

It's at this moment that an extraordinary feeling waves over me. I'm aware that I'm standing with my brother-in-law, Mark, at the boundary in the same spot, but I'm also enraptured, in some kind of a trance even, by what is unfolding on the pitch.

I can feel the hard leather in my hand, the quality hand-stitching of the seam on the worn Dukes ball. I can feel the smoothness of one side, the roughness on the other, sense the gold lettering of the maker. I catch the aroma of linseed in the air from the bat. It's as if I'm right there on that pitch, holding the ball in my hand getting a pep talk from Chaz, I can hear his words softly in my ear, relaxing me, inspiring me, filling my head with confidence, making me focus on the moment. I'm looking on towards the church, down the wicket at a crowd of people and at my older self. Everything is so vivid, I can see everything as clear as if I was looking through a magnifying glass. Everything seems to have slowed down, almost stood still.

It's an odd feeling that I'm yet to explain. Mark said that my eyes seemed to have glazed over and he was patting me on the shoulder and I appeared so engrossed by the game that he gave up trying to get my attention. But I do know that I was aware that Mark was there and could hear what he was saying.

Forth runs in for the fourth ball of the over and it's a deceptive shorter ball, which Robinson moves out to meet, but it's longer than he thinks and can only manage to scramble the ball for a one. He's lost strike which gives Whiston a slightly better chance. But there's still a slugger at the crease who can smell the glory a boundary would give him. He only needs two runs but you can sense by the look on his face that he wants to go for it. Chaz comes in again to speak to Nick, he whispers quietly words of confidence, words the crowd or the other fielders couldn't quite hear, but I know what he says in Nick's ear and that one word is the one which sticks in young Nick's head. It must surely have been this that inspired Nick for what came next.

Forth walks a little further out than before for his run up this time. He's facing Lee Coulbeck, a great, powerful bowler and built like the proverbial brick shit house, with forearms like a farmer's. He's going to whack this out of the ground and into the church yard if he makes clean contact. As Nick starts his run up he tries to suppress the feelings of doubt that are entering his head. He tries not to think about his boss at the *Advertiser* telling him off for being late on Monday, or his mates taking the piss out of him for not being able to take his ale. He tries to remember the words that Chaz just said to him, he focusses for the most important ball he's ever sent down that wicket. There's one word in particular which just keeps repeating in his head, in my head, in time with his strides, in time with the thumping of his feet on the sun-baked pitch. He comes in at full pelt and whips his arm over, holding the shiny red of the leather cricket ball to his right side and lofts it, just slightly later than his usual pitch, and in it goes. The whole crowd watch the scene, as if the world is all in complete slooooow mooootiooon and in it comes towards Coulbeck, who adjusts his feet like a baseball slugger to meet the short pitched ball. But, again, it's deceptive. It's not as short as Coulbeck thinks and he hastily has to stab down to the ground to cover his feet. But this ball not only has swing but also has pace and goes under him taking the off stump out, which then summersaults twice, three times, both bails spin and whistle through the air as Nick, Chaz behind him, and me at the boundary say in unison,

"YORKER!"

*"Good scores are valuable, but centuries stick in the mind... it has its own magic."* Geoffrey Boycott, Yorkshire cricketer.

# Mason's Clock

THE CROWD PILE onto the pitch in their absolute delight.

"Nick's only gone and got 'im with a superb Yorker!" cries one.

The euphoria of the moment is tangible for all. It's as if England have won the World Cup against New Zealand, or the Ashes in 1953, and '81, against all the odds, all rolled into one. Old men, young boys and teenagers dance and skip across the pitch, all wanting to share the triumph they've just witnessed. Even Carl, the groundsman, runs on clapping and cheering, not caring a jot at that moment about all the extra work the pitch invasion was causing him!

"Fantastic win lads, wonderful to watch. Best game in years. You did it fo' Whiston boys! Why can't we do that every week?" he says while raising his arms in the air; and then, as if regaining his senses, "...mind that wicket though you lot, come on now,"

Chaz is picked up by some of the young men in the crowd, as is young Nick. They hold them aloft as the people all about them cheer and wave, throwing their hats in the air. They're just so elated that they don't know what to do, or say other than just laugh and punch the air with sheer joy.

"This is better than if The Millers had won t' FA Cup!" someone shouts; and at that moment they mean it too.

Brother-in-law, Mark, and I just instinctively hug each other. "Did you see that last bowl?.." says Mark "...I wondered if you were still there for a moment..." he says, referring to my trance-like state presumably, "...you had me worried there!"

"Oh, I was there, right there, I saw it alright..." says I, and I knew that it was much deeper than that, that I'd had a feeling of being right there on the pitch.

Or, at least, almost right there. This feeling, at the time, I couldn't put into words until a strong urge came over me to do so by recording the events here and to, hopefully, go some way to explain what happened that day, as fantastical as it may seem to anyone of sound mind. I'm too sensible to think that it was real, but it certainly felt real at the time. It's hard to put into words happenings that we just can't comprehend unless we start sounding like psychics or believers in the paranormal. Certainly I have never been of such a persuasion.

"...lets go find the girls..." I say, snapping back into my normal self.

The Cleethorpes batsmen trudge off back to the pavilion, almost unnoticed in the euphoria around them, as they lick their wounds. The scoreboard keeper, Colin Black, that silhouetted figure in the distance, has just flicked over the number to show the final result at stumps:

Away Team 200
10 wickets
39.5 overs.

It's official Whiston have won by 1 run.

"See I told thee, this side can beat anyone on t' right day!" says the old man who'd done nothing but doubt his team for all but the last four overs. His friend gives him a knowing look but he's over joyed so nothing matters. Right at that moment, for all those fans, for everyone watching from Whiston, for me and my family, all the troubles in the world are completely forgotten about.

All that mattered was that team, that score, that Yorker.

As the excitement slowly simmered down, Chaz was placed back down.

"It's great to be 'ome after all this time." One spectator thought they heard him say. But his voice was being lost among the cheering and laughter.

"That bar'll do well t' neet, that's fo' sure!" someone joked and, indeed, people who hadn't been near the Shed for many years came pouring in, ordering rounds of drinks with gay abandon which, as we all know, is completely out of character for any self-respecting Yorkshireman! Such was their utter delight.

Young Nick, the other hero at only 19 years old, was grinning from ear to ear as he was carried into the clubhouse, as if on the crest of a wave.

Chaz was still receiving adoring adulation as he wandered over to the boundary off to the right hand side of the ground. I could just about make out that he was talking to an elegant slim lady, wearing a floral summer dress, in her mid-thirties perhaps, who was smiling at him in wonderment.

"I knew you could do it... it's lovely to see you back here. It's been a while hasn't it Chaz!" She said, clearly besotted with him.

Some in the crowd near them saw them talking and heard that he'd said something to her about where they could meet up; later that evening maybe, they thought.

"See you under Mason's Clock at 7..." something like that but he definitely mentioned Mason's Clock.

"That's in Town isn't it?" A spectator said to his friend.

"Aye, it's where the jewellers is but the clock's been gone donkey's years 'ant it?" said his pal.

"Nay, I think they've put a new 'un there..." he replied.

And, as they drank on the pavilion terrace and in the bar, and down on the boundary, the music started playing and the sun came out full once more on that late September evening as if in recognition of that wonderful day's cricket. The magnificent, brilliant white church tower peered down on them all, as if guarding everyone and keeping a watchful eye on them. Captain Garth Page was surrounded by hungry cricket fans desperate for the low down on how the team pulled it off, hanging on his every word. Garth Page caught sight of Chaz in the distance, as did I at the very same moment. He waved to him, but Chaz didn't see him.

Chaz had gone over to thank Colin Black the scorekeeper like a true gent. Colin put his arm around him, as if they were old long lost friends. They patted each other and joked and smiled and then, as the sun shone against the edge of the side screen, glinting as it went lower in the sky, the two figures became blurry and shimmered almost like a mirage in the distance. Garth Page noticed this, as did I, and so must other onlookers have, on that glorious day. I don't know where they went but, as the sun began to set, blurring them from sight it was almost as if, in that moment, they just disappeared. But I'm sure it must just have been a trick of the light. I'm just too sensible to think that it could've been anything other.

∼

# A Century, Not Out

LATER ON, AS THE SUN WAS JUST GOING DOWN on that lovely day, still with a pint of golden ale in my hand, I looked at all those pictures on the walls again, of the old teams from similar glorious cricketing days gone by and I wondered about how well they had played and if, maybe, some of their grandchildren and great grandchildren still played. It seemed timeless, stretching back many generations of Whiston folk, continuing for many more. Maybe some of those faces, or ones like them were out there today. It was then that I noticed one newspaper clipping from a 1950 issue of the *Sheffield Star* with a picture that sent a shiver down my spine. It was framed, amongst a montage of other clippings. Squinting to get a closer look at the caption, I moved my head close up to it. I could scarcely believe what I was seeing…

**"Whiston PCCC in Dramatic Finale,"** went the main headline
*"…New Star All-rounder…."* It continued, *"…CP R…Richa?…"*

I couldn't fully make it out, but it then went on:

*"…bowled 6 wickets for 37, and 100 not out."*

The photograph and short article underneath were faded and grainy so I couldn't quite read the whole thing but I could make out some of it. There was an almost uncanny resemblance to the star of today's cricket match. Perhaps in the photo he had much more hair, but this man was still thin on top, he was raising a pint in front of him, so his face was partially obscured. But it was enough to stop me in my tracks. It couldn't have been though because this was a seventy year old newspaper clipping, so the only logical explanation must've been that the Yorkshire ale was playing tricks with my mind. That must've been it.

"Dad?" I whispered to myself, whilst shaking my head in disbelief, as I tried to see the picture more clearly. Oh, how I wished it were true though! After all, we had all witnessed some quite extraordinary events out there on the cricket pitch that day. Some fabulous cricket, glorious sunshine, a thousand fans who seemed to flock from all over the village and beyond to watch the game; and a win against all the odds. I shook my head some more to bring myself back to my senses and my thoughts were broken by a familiar voice.

"Come on then Our Mark." Our Anne called out "…bet you're glad you stayed till the end …we were all wondering where you'd got to, we're ready for the off."

As we wandered back to the Tesla in the carpark, homeward bound, in the fading evening light on that very special late summer's day, I could've sworn that I heard a skylark singing its heart out as it had done earlier in the day. I looked around to where the sweet sound was coming from. I gazed high in the sky, towards The Bench and over the hedgerows but could only see the beautiful red sunset over Church Fields.

The End